THE TEMPEST

WILLIAM SHAKESPEARE

www.realreads.co.uk

Retold by Helen Street
Illustrated by Charly Cheung

Published by Real Reads Ltd
Stroud, Gloucestershire, UK
www.realreads.co.uk

First published in 2010

ISBN 978-1-906230-46-3

Printed in China by Imago Ltd
Designed by Lucy Guenot
Typeset by Bookcraft Ltd, Stroud, Gloucestershire

CONTENTS

THE CHARACTERS

Prospero and Miranda

Prospero's powerful magic creates a storm. What does he plan for the survivors who wash ashore on his island? And what surprises will the storm bring to Miranda, his daughter?

Alonso and Ferdinand

Alonso, King of Naples, and his son Ferdinand, both think the other has drowned in the storm. Will father and son find each other again?

Gonzalo

This kind-hearted counsellor tries to look on the bright side. Will his good nature lead him into danger, or will it save his life?

Stephano and Trinculo

These two drunkards want to take over the island, but can they stop drinking long enough to carry out their plan?

Antonio and Sebastian

Long ago Antonio, now Duke of Milan, betrayed his brother Prospero and stole his dukedom. Will he persuade Sebastian to steal *his* brother Alonso's kingdom?

Caliban

Prospero's slave must bear the punishments his master gives him. Will he find someone to help him carry out his desperate plan?

Ariel

Ariel is a spirit, and a faithful servant to Prospero, but he yearns for one thing – his freedom. Will he earn it?

5

THE TEMPEST

ACT ONE, SCENE ONE
ON BOARD THE KING OF
NAPLES' SHIP, IN A STORM

Master

Bosun!

Bosun

Here, Master.

Master

Bestir the mariners, and look lively, or we run
ourselves aground.

Bosun

Jump to, me hearties! Take in the top sail.
Blow till thou burst, thou wind.

> *Alonso, Sebastian, Antonio and Gonzalo
> come on deck.*

Alonso

Good Bosun, where's the Master?

Bosun

I pray you now, keep below.

Antonio

Where is the Master, Bosun?

7

Bosun

Do you not hear him? You mar our labour.
Keep to your cabins.

Gonzalo

Nay, be patient.

Bosun

When the sea is! Enough! To your cabins and
trouble us not.

Gonzalo

Good man, yet remember whom thou hast aboard.

Bosun

None that I love more dearly than myself.
You're a counsellor. If you can make peace with this
storm, I'll not do a thing more. If you cannot, then
give thanks you have lived so long. Now, out of our
way, I say!

Alonso, Sebastian, Antonio and Gonzalo go below.

Down with the topmast! Lower away!

Shouts from below.

A plague upon this howling: they are louder
than the weather.

Sebastian, Antonio and Gonzalo come back on deck.

Yet again? What do you want now?

Shall we stop our labours and drown?

Have you a mind to sink?

Sebastian

Mind your tongue, you good-for-nothing dog!

Bosun

Work you then.

Antonio

You insolent noisemaker! We are less afraid to
be drowned than thou art.

Bosun

Lay her a-hold, a-hold! Set her two courses off to
sea again.

Some bedraggled sailors enter.

Sailors

All's lost! Say your prayers!

Gonzalo

The King and Prince are saying theirs. Let's join
with them.

Antonio

We are cheated of our lives by these drunkards and
this bawling rascal.

May you drown ten times o'er!

Sailors

Mercy on us!

We split, we split! Farewell, my wife and children.

Farewell, brother. We split, we split, we split!

Antonio

Let's all sink with the King.

Sebastian

Let's take our leave of him.

Gonzalo

Now would I give a thousand furlongs of sea, for
an acre of barren land, long heath, brown furze,
anything. The will above be done! But I would fain
die a dry death.

ACT ONE, SCENE TWO
THE ISLAND, IN FRONT OF
PROSPERO'S CAVE

Miranda

If by thy art, my dearest father, you have
Put the wild waters in this roar, allay them.
The sky, it seems, would pour down stinking pitch
But that the sea, mounting to the clouds above,
Dashes the fire out. O, I have suffered
With those that I saw suffer: a brave vessel
Dashed all to pieces. O, the cry did knock
Against my very heart: poor souls, they perished.

Prospero

Be not distressed, but tell your piteous heart
There's no harm done.

Miranda

O, woe the day.

Prospero

No harm. I have done nothing, but in care of thee,
Of thee, my dear one, thee my daughter, who
Art ignorant of what thou art, not knowing
That I am more than Prospero, master
Of this poor cave and father to thee.

Miranda

More to know
Did never meddle with my thoughts.

Prospero

'Tis time
I should inform thee further. Lend thy hand
And pluck my magic garment from me. So.

Prospero lays down his cloak.

Wipe thou thine eyes. The wreck which touched thy heart,
Was by enchantment done, in such a way
That not a single soul was lost, or harmed.
Obey, and be attentive. Can'st thou remember
A time before we came unto this place?

Miranda

Certainly sir, I can, though 'tis far off,
And rather like a dream, but had I not
Four or five women once, that tended me?

Prospero

Thou had'st, and more, Miranda. Twelve years since,
Thy father was the Duke of Milan and
A Prince of power.

Miranda

Sir, are you not my father?

Prospero

Indeed, thou art my daughter, but attend.
Those many years ago when I was Duke,
My thoughts were always tending to my books,
And so in charge of state affairs I put
My brother, and thy uncle, Antonio.
And thus neglected much my worldly life.
In my false brother, an evil nature grew.
He did believe he was the Duke, and so
In secret did he plot with Naples' King
To turn me out of mine own dukedom.
And then one night, did Antonio open
The gates of Milan and in the darkness
Did hurry me hence with thy crying self.

Miranda

Wherefore did they not that hour destroy us?

Prospero

Well demanded, wench.
So dear the love my people bore me, child,
They did not dare. Instead, they set us on
A leaky boat with neither sail nor mast
And left us to the mercy of the sea.

Miranda

How came we ashore?

Prospero

By providence divine,
Some food we had, and some fresh water, that
A noble Neapolitan, Gonzalo,
Out of his charity did give us, with
Rich garments, linens, stuffs and necessaries.
Knowing I loved my books, he furnished me
From mine own library with volumes that
I prize above my dukedom.

Miranda

Would I might but ever see that man.
And now, good sir, I pray you, your reason
For raising this sea-storm?

Prospero

Know you this much:
By accident most strange hath kind fortune
Brought to this shore mine enemies. But now
These questions cease. Thou art inclined to sleep.
Give in to it. I know thou canst not choose.

Miranda falls asleep.

Come away, servant, come, I am ready now.
Approach, my Ariel, come!

Ariel enters.

Ariel
All hail, great master, grave sir, hail: I come
To answer thy best pleasure; be it to fly,
To swim, to dive into the fire, to ride
On the curled clouds; to thy strong bidding,
Set Ariel your task.

Prospero

Hast thou, my spirit,

Performed the tempest as I ordered thee?

Ariel

In every detail.

With lightning bolts and dreadful thunderclaps,

I stirred the storm, and mighty Neptune did

Make bold his waves about the royal ship.

And every soul aboard the trembling bark

Did feel a fever of the mad. All but

The sailors plunged into the foaming brine.

The King's son, Ferdinand, with hair on end,

Was the first man that leaped, crying 'Hell

Is empty and all the devils are here!'

Prospero

But are they safe?

Ariel

Not a hair perished. And as thou bad'st me

In groups I have dispersed them about the isle.

The King's son have I landed by himself,

Where now he sits, his arms in this sad knot.

Prospero

And of the ship itself?

Ariel

Safe in harbour.

The mariners all under hatches stowed,

Who, with a charm, I have left all asleep.

Prospero

Thou hast done well, but there is more to do.

Now make thyself invisible. Go hence.

Ariel leaves.

Awake, dear heart, awake!

Thou hast slept well, awake!

Miranda

The strangeness of your story, put

Heaviness in me.

Prospero

Shake it off; come on.

We'll visit Caliban, my slave, who never

Yields us kind answer.

Miranda

'Tis a villain, sir, I do not like to look on.

Prospero

But as 'tis,

We cannot miss him; he does make our fire,

Fetch in our wood, and serves in other ways.

Come forth now, Caliban, come forth, slave.

Caliban *(inside the cave)*

There's wood enough within.

Prospero

Come forth, I say. There's other business for thee.

Caliban

A slimy fog drop on you both, I say.

Prospero

For this be sure, tonight thou shalt have cramps.

Thou shalt be pinched as thick as honeycomb,

Each pinch more stinging than the sting of bees.

Caliban

This island's mine, by Sycorax my mother,
Which thou tak'st from me. When thou cam'st first
Thou strokest me and made much of me;
Then I did love thee.
Cursed be I that did so. All the charms
Of Sycorax, toads, beetles, bats light on you.

Prospero

Ungrateful creature,
With human care did I use thee, lodged thee
In mine own cave, 'til thou did try to seize
My daughter from me, vile thing that thou art.
Now fetch us in more fuel, and be thou quick.

Caliban

I must obey, such is his power o'er me.

*Caliban leaves. Ariel enters, invisible; he is singing
and playing a flute. Ariel is followed by Ferdinand,
the King of Naples' son.*

Ariel

Full fathom five thy father lies;
Of his bones are corals made;
Those are pearls that were his eyes;
Nothing of him that doth fade

But doth suffer a sea-change
Into something rich and strange.
Sea nymphs hourly ring his knell.
Hark now I hear them. Ding, dong, bell.

Ferdinand
This sweet, sad song reminds me of the King,
My father, who has surely drowned at sea.

Prospero
The fringed curtains of thine eye advance
And say what thou seest here.

Miranda
Is it a spirit, sir?

Prospero
No, wench, it eats, and sleeps, and hath such senses
As we. Though somewhat stained with grief, he is
A fair example of a man.

Miranda
O, I would say he is a thing divine.

Prospero *(to Ariel)*
My plan begins to work. I'll free thee, spirit,
Within two days for this.

Ferdinand

The island's goddess this must surely be!

Miranda

No goddess, sir, but just a mortal maid.

Ferdinand

O, I would you the Queen of Naples make,

For this cruel tempest makes a king of me.

Prospero *(to himself)*

They love each other at first sight, but yet

Too light winning may make the prize seem light.

(to Ferdinand)

'Tis my belief that thou hast put thyself
Upon this island, as a spy, to win it
From me, the lord of it.

Ferdinand

I assure you, sir, that is not so!

Miranda

In such a man there can be only good!

Prospero

Speak not for him; he's a traitor. Come.
(to Ferdinand)
I'll manacle thy neck and feet together;
Sea-water shalt thou drink, thy food shall be
But withered roots.

Ferdinand

I will resist.

Prospero

My power is stronger
For I can here disarm thee with this stick.

Prospero waves his staff.
Ferdinand is enchanted and cannot move.

Miranda

O father, I beseech you, for he's gentle.

Prospero
Hence! Hang not on my garments.

Miranda
Sir, have pity.

Prospero
Be still, for one word more shall anger me.

Miranda *(to Ferdinand)*
Be of comfort,
My father's of a better nature, sir,
Than he appears by speech.

Prospero
Speak not with him, Miranda, follow me.

ACT TWO, SCENE ONE
ELSEWHERE ON THE ISLAND

Alonso, Sebastian, Antonio and Gonzalo
are wandering about.

Gonzalo *(to Alonso)*
Beseech you, sir, be merry. You have cause.
For our escape is much beyond our loss.

Alonso
Prithee, peace.

Sebastian *(to Antonio)*
He receives comfort like cold porridge.

Gonzalo
Though this island seem to be deserted,
Uninhabitable and inaccessible,
The air breathes upon us here most sweetly.

Sebastian
It smells to me no better than a bog.

Gonzalo
Here is everything advantageous to life.

Antonio
Except the means to live.

Gonzalo

And one thing more that is most strange, I think,
Our garments now are fresh as when we first
Did put them on in Naples.

Alonso

Peace! Enough!
My son and heir is lost, my Ferdinand.
O what strange fish hath made his meal on thee?

Gonzalo

He yet may live. I saw him beat the waves.

Ariel, invisible, enters and plays sweet music.

My eyes are heavy with the weight of sleep.

Alonso

Mine, also.

Antonio

We two, my lord,
Will guard your person, while you take your rest.

Gonzalo and Alonso fall asleep.

Sebastian

What a strange drowsiness possesses them!

Antonio

It is the quality of the climate.

Sebastian

I do not find myself disposed to sleep.

Antonio

Nor I. They dropped as by a thunderbolt.

What if, my worthy friend? I say, what if?

My strong imagination sees a crown

Dropping upon thy head.

Sebastian

What dost thou mean?

Antonio

You grant your nephew Ferdinand is dead?

Sebastian

I do.

Antonio

Then tell me, who's the next heir of Naples?

Sebastian

That would be me.

Antonio

Say this were death that now hath seized them,
You would be king and no one else would know.

Sebastian

'Tis true, and now I do remember how
You did supplant your brother, Prospero.

Antonio

And look how well my garments sit upon me.
Here lies your brother,
No better than the earth he lies upon.
This dagger here will turn your fortunes round.

Sebastian

Thou hast persuaded me. As thou got'st Milan,
I'll come by Naples. Draw thy sword. One stroke
And I, the king, shall love thee.

Antonio

Draw together;
And when I rear my hand, do you the like
To fall it on Gonzalo.

Ariel

My master through his art foresees the danger
That you, his friend, are in, and sends me forth
To keep you living.

Ariel sings in Gonzalo's ear and wakes him up.

Gonzalo

Now, good angels preserve the King.

Alonso *(waking)*

Why are you drawn?

Sebastian

Whiles we stood here securing your repose,
We heard a hollow burst of bellowing
Like bulls, or rather lions. Did it not wake you?

Alonso

I heard nothing.

Antonio

O,'twas a din to fright a monster's ear;
To make an earthquake; sure it was the roar
Of a whole herd of lions.

Alonso

Heard you this, Gonzalo?

Gonzalo

Upon my honour, sir, I heard a humming.
'Tis best, methinks, we stand upon our guard.

Alonso

Lead off this ground, and let's make further search
For my poor son.

They leave with weapons drawn.

ACT TWO, SCENE TWO
ANOTHER PART OF THE ISLAND

Caliban is gathering sticks.

Caliban

All the infections that are under the sun
On Prospero fall and slowly eat him up.
I know his spirits he will set on me,
To pinch me, fright me, pitch me in the mire
Or lead me in the dark out of my way.

Trinculo enters.

Here comes a spirit of his, and to torment me
For bringing wood in slowly: I'll fall flat;
Perchance he will not notice me.

Trinculo

Here's neither bush, nor shrub to bear off any
weather at all; and another storm brewing. If it
should thunder, as it did before, I know not
where to hide my head.

He sees Caliban under his cloak on the ground.

What have we here, a man or a fish? Dead or alive? A fish, he smells like a fish. But he's legged like a man and his fins are like arms. This is no fish, but an islander that hath lately suffered from a thunderbolt.

Alas, the storm is come again. My best way is to creep under his cloak; there is no other shelter hereabouts.

Trinculo hides under the cloak with Caliban as Stephano enters, drunk.

Caliban
Do not torment me. O!

Stephano

What's the matter? Have we devils here? I have not escaped drowning, to be afeard now of your four legs. Not while Stephano still breathes.

Caliban

The spirit torments me. O!

Stephano

This is some monster of the isle, with four legs. Where the devil should he learn our language? If I can keep him tame and get to Naples with him, he's a present for any emperor.

Caliban

I'll bring my wood home faster.

Stephano

He shall taste of my bottle. Open your mouth.

Trinculo

I should know that voice; it should be – but he is drowned, and these are devils. O, defend me!

Stephano

Four legs and two voices, a most interesting monster. I will pour some in thy other mouth.

Trinculo

Stephano, I am Trinculo, thy good friend. But
art thou not drowned, Stephano?

Trinculo jumps up and hugs Stephano.

Stephano

Prithee do not turn me about, my stomach is
not constant.

Caliban *(to himself)*

These be fine things, and if they be not sprites,
he's a brave god who gives me this heavenly
liquor. I will kneel to him.

(to Stephano)

Hast thou not dropped from heaven?

Stephano

Yes, out of the moon!

Caliban

I'll show thee every fertile inch of the island, and
I will kiss thy foot; I prithee, be my god. I'll swear
myself thy subject.

Stephano

Come on then, down and swear.

Caliban

I'll show thee the best springs, I'll pluck thee berries.
I'll fish for thee and get thee wood enough.
A plague upon the tyrant that I serve.
I'll bear him no more sticks, but follow thee,
Thou wondrous man.

Trinculo

A most ridiculous monster, to make a wonder
of a poor drunkard.

Stephano

I prithee now, lead the way without any more talking.
Trinculo, the King and all our company being
drowned, we will inherit here.

Caliban *(sings drunkenly as if to Prospero)*

Farewell master, farewell, farewell.

Stephano

O, brave monster! Lead the way.

ACT THREE, SCENE ONE
OUTSIDE PROSPERO'S CAVE

Ferdinand enters, carrying a log.

Ferdinand

I must remove some thousands of these logs,
And pile them up on pain of punishment.
But I am glad to labour so because
The mistress that I serve has smiled at me.

Miranda enters, with Prospero watching out of sight.

Miranda

Alas, now pray you,
Work not so hard: I would the lightning had
Burnt up those logs that you are forced to pile.
Pray set it down, and rest you; when this burns,
'Twill weep for having wearied you. My father
Is hard at study. Pray now rest yourself.

Ferdinand

The sun will set before I shall discharge
What I must strive to do, sweet mistress.

Miranda

If you'll sit down,

I'll bear your logs a while. Pray give me that;

I'll take it to the pile.

Ferdinand

No, precious creature,

I had rather crack my sinews, break my back,

Than you should such dishonour undergo,

While I sit lazy by.

Miranda

You look wearily.

Ferdinand

No, noble mistress, 'tis fresh morning with me
When you are here. Yet, I do beseech you,
Chiefly, that I might set it in my prayers,
What is your name?

Miranda

Miranda. O, my father,
I have broken my promise by saying so.

Ferdinand

Admired Miranda,
Indeed the top of admiration, worth
What's dearest to the world. Full many a lady
Have I liked, but you, o you, so perfect,
So lovely – they could not compare to thee.

Miranda

And for myself, I would not wish
Any companion in the world but you.

Ferdinand

I am in my condition
A prince, Miranda, I do think a king.

The very instant that I saw you, did
My heart fly to your side, and for your sake
Am I this patient log man.

Miranda
Do you love me?

Ferdinand
O, I do love, prize and honour you.

Miranda
I am your wife, if you will marry me.
You may deny me, but I'll be your servant
Whether you will or no.

Ferdinand
My mistress, dearest, here is my hand.

Miranda
And mine, with my heart in it. And now farewell,
Till half an hour hence.

They go out separately.

Prospero
I see they are in love, and I am glad,
But yet, ere supper-time, must I perform
Much business, so I'll to my books.

ACT THREE, SCENE TWO
ELSEWHERE ON THE ISLAND

Caliban

Now wilt thou listen to my plan?

Stephano

Indeed, I will.

Ariel, invisible to them, enters.

Caliban

As I told thee before, I am subject to a tyrant,
a sorcerer, that by his cunning hath cheated me
of the island.

Ariel

Thou liest.

Caliban *(to Trinculo)*

Thou liest, thou jesting monkey, thou.
I would my valiant master would destroy thee!
I do not lie.

Stephano

Trinculo, if you trouble him any more, I will
supplant some of your teeth.

Trinculo
Why, I said nothing.

Stephano
Mum then, and no more. Proceed.

Caliban
I say by sorcery he got this isle from me, but if thou dar'st do what I ask, thou shalt be lord of it and I will serve thee.

41

Stephano
How shall this be done?

Caliban
I'll take thee to him when he is asleep,
Where thou mayst knock a nail into his head.

Ariel
Thou liest, thou canst not.

Caliban *(to Trinculo)*
Thou scurvy patch!

(to Stephano)
I do beseech thy greatness, give him blows.

Stephano
Trinculo, interrupt the monster one word further,
and by this hand, I'll make mincemeat out of thee.

Trinculo
Why, what did I? I did nothing.

Stephano
Didst thou not say he lied?

Ariel
Thou liest.

Stephano *(to Trinculo)*
Do I so? Take thou that.

He hits Trinculo

Caliban

Beat him enough and then I'll beat him, too.

Stephano

Now forward with your tale.

Caliban

Why, as I told thee, 'tis a custom with him
In the afternoon to sleep; there thou may'st brain him
Having first seized his books; or with a log
Batter his skull, or stab him with a stake,
Or cut his throat with thy knife. Remember
First to take his books, for he is powerless
Without them.

Stephano

Monster, I will kill this man; his daughter and I
will be king and queen; and Trinculo and thyself
shall be viceroys. Dost thou like the plot, Trinculo?

Trinculo

Excellent.

Stephano

Give me thy hand. I am sorry I beat thee.

Caliban

Within this half hour will he be asleep.
Wilt thou destroy him then?

Stephano
Ay, on my honour.

Ariel (to himself)
This will I tell my master.

Strange music is heard.

Caliban
Be not afeard, the isle is full of noises,
Sounds, and sweet airs, that give delight and hurt not.

Sometimes, a thousand twangling instruments
Will hum about mine ears; and sometimes voices,
That if I then had waked after long sleep,
Will make me sleep again, and then in dreaming,
The clouds methought would open and show riches
Ready to drop upon me that, when I waked,
I cried to dream again.

Stephano
This will prove a fine kingdom for me.

Caliban
When Prospero is destroyed.

Stephano
That shall be by and by.

Trinculo
The sound is going away, let's follow it and after do
our work.

45

ACT FOUR, SCENE ONE
OUTSIDE PROSPERO'S CAVE

Prospero enters with Ferdinand and Miranda.

Prospero

If I have too severely punished you,
Your compensation makes amends, for I
Have given you here a third of mine own life.
I give her hand to thee. All thy vexations
Were but my trials of thy love, and thou
Hast bravely stood the test.

*A masque is performed by Prospero's spirits
to entertain the young couple.*

Ferdinand

This is a most majestic vision, sir.
May I be bold to think that these are spirits?

Prospero

They are, and all of them at my command.

Ferdinand

O, let me live here ever, for wonders
Such as these, make this place a paradise.

The masque suddenly ends when Prospero speaks.

Prospero

I had forgot that foul conspiracy
Of the beast Caliban and his confederates
Against my life. The moment of their plot
Is almost come. Enough, my spirits, go!

The spirits go.

Our revels now are ended; these our actors
(As I foretold you) were all spirits, and
Are melted into air, into thin air.
And like the ghostly nature of this vision,
The cloud-capped towers, the gorgeous palaces,
The solemn temples, the great globe itself,
Yea, everything upon it, shall dissolve
And leave not a wisp behind. We are such stuff
As dreams are made of, and our little life
Is rounded with a sleep.
Go rest yourselves a while inside the cave.

Ferdinand and Miranda go off into the cave.

Come, Ariel.

Ariel appears.

Ariel

What's thy pleasure?

Prospero

Spirit, we must prepare to meet with Caliban.
Say again, where didst thou leave these varlets?

Ariel

I charmed their ears that they would follow me.
Through pricking briers and jagged thorns they came,
Until I left them in some stinking bog.

Prospero

Go bring the fancy costumes from my cave;
We'll hang them out as bait to catch these thieves.

*Ariel goes and quickly returns with fine clothes that he and
Prospero hang about the place. They hide when Caliban,
Stephano and Trinculo enter.*

Caliban

Pray you tread softly, we now are near his cave.

Stephano

Monster, that music did lead us a merry dance.

Trinculo

And I do smell somewhat foul.

Caliban

Prithee, my king, be quiet. See'st thou here,

This is the mouth of his cave. No noise, and enter.

Do that good mischief, which may make this island

Thine own for ever, and I thy Caliban,

For aye thy foot-licker.

Trinculo *(seeing the clothes)*

O worthy Stephano, look what a wardrobe

here is for thee.

Trinculo tries on a robe.

Caliban

Let it alone thou fool, it is but trash.

Stephano

Take off that gown, Trinculo, it shall be mine.

Trinculo

Thy grace shall have it.

Caliban

Let's do the murder first; if he awake,

From toe to crown he'll fill our skins with pinches.

Stephano

Be you quiet, monster. And I shall have this one,

and this, and this. Here's one for you, Trinculo.

Trinculo

Come, monster, take the rest.

Caliban

I will have none of it. We shall lose our time,

And all be turned to barnacles, or to apes.

Stephano

Monster, help to bear this away, or I will turn you out

of my kingdom. Go to, carry this.

Trinculo

And this.

Stephano

Yes, and this.

They pile up clothes on Caliban, then spirits in the shape of dogs appear and chase them off. Prospero and Ariel reappear.

Prospero

Let them be hunted soundly. At this hour

Lie at my mercy all mine enemies.

Shortly shall all my labours end, and thou,

My spirit, shalt have from me thy freedom.

ACT FIVE, SCENE ONE
OUTSIDE PROSPERO'S CAVE

Prospero enters wearing his magic robe, with Ariel.

Prospero
How fares the King and all his followers?

Ariel
I have confined them as you did command.
They cannot budge; your charm so strongly works 'em,
That if you now beheld them, your affections
Would become tender.

Prospero
Dost thou think so, spirit?

Ariel
Mine would, sir, were I human.

Prospero
And mine shall. Go, release them, Ariel.
My charms I'll break, their senses I'll restore
And they shall be themselves.

Ariel
I'll fetch them, sir.

Ariel leaves.

Prospero

I have bedimmed the noontide sun, called forth
Rebellious winds; to rattling thunder
Have I given fire, and split the mighty oaks
With lightning bolts. But this rough magic now
I do renounce. And this, my staff, I'll break
And bury deep beneath the earth. Then last,
Into the sea I'll throw my sacred book.

*Ariel returns, leading Alonso, Gonzalo, Sebastian and
Antonio under a spell. He leaves them in a circle that
Prospero has drawn on the ground.*

Prospero

Most cruelly did thou, Alonso, use me,
As did my brother, who with Sebastian
Would here have killed their king; I do forgive thee,
Unnatural though thou art. The charm dissolves.

Alonso and his followers come to their senses again.

Prospero

Behold sir king, the wronged Duke of Milan, Prospero.
I bid thee hearty welcome.

Alonso

If thou be'st Prospero, I do entreat
Thou pardon me my wrongs; but how should
Prospero be living, and be here, upon this shore
Where I have lost my dear son Ferdinand?

Prospero

I grieve with you, for I have lost a daughter;
In this same tempest was she lost to me.

Alonso

Alas, if only they were living now,
At home in Naples, as the king and queen.

Prospero

But look, I pray you sir, within my cave.

*Prospero reveals Ferdinand and Miranda
playing chess within the cave.*

Ferdinand *(seeing Alonso)*

Though the seas threaten, they are merciful
And I have cursed them without cause.

Alonso

Now all the blessings of a glad father,
Compass thee about.

Father and son embrace.

Miranda

O wonder!

How many goodly creatures are there here!

How beauteous mankind is! O brave new world

That has such people in it.

Alonso

What is this maid with whom thou wast at play?

Ferdinand

Sir, she is daughter to this noble duke

And she shall be my own if you allow.

Alonso

Give me your hands.

Let grief and sorrow still embrace his heart

That doth not wish you joy.

Prospero

Sirs, I invite you all to rest yourselves

This night within my cave and there

I'll tell the story of my life. Then shall

I bring you to your ship, and so to Naples,

Where I have hope to see the nuptial

Of these, our dear beloved, solemnised.

Ariel, your work and mine is done. Now go

And to the elements be free. Farewell.

TAKING THINGS FURTHER

The real read

This *Real Reads* version of *The Tempest* is a retelling of William Shakespeare's magnificent work. If you would like to read the full play in all its original splendour, many complete editions are available, from bargain paperbacks to beautifully-bound hardbacks. You should find a copy in your local bookshop or library, or even a charity shop.

Filling in the spaces

The loss of so many of William Shakespeare's original words is a sad but necessary part of the shortening process. We have had to make some difficult decisions, omitting subplots and details, some important, some less so, but all interesting. We have also, at times, taken the liberty of combining two events into one, or of giving a character words or actions that originally belong to another. The points below will fill in some of the gaps, but nothing can beat the original.

- At the beginning of the story, the King's ship is on its way back to Naples from Tunis in Africa, where the King and his noblemen went for the wedding of the King's daughter.

- Before Prospero and Miranda came to the island, a witch called Sycorax lived there. She imprisoned Ariel inside a tree. Ariel was trapped in the tree for twelve years before Prospero came. Prospero freed him from the spell, and made him his servant.

- Before Sycorax died she had a son, Caliban, who was left alone on the island. When Prospero and his daughter arrived, they took pity on Caliban, treating him well and teaching him how to speak their language.

- Prospero had promised to free Ariel from being his servant, but when Ariel reminds him of the promise he gets angry because he has more work for Ariel to do.

- When Prospero's brother, Antonio, was plotting to overthrow him, Antonio asked the King of Naples for help in return for a yearly sum of money.

- Gonzalo gives a speech about how he would rule the island if he was king.

- While Alonso, Gonzalo and the others are searching for Ferdinand, a magic banquet appears in front of them. By this time they are very hungry. Just as they are about to eat, however, the banquet disappears, and Ariel, disguised as a harpy, tells Alonso, Antonio and Sebastian what wicked men they are for turning Prospero out of his dukedom.

- When Prospero's spirits put on a masque to entertain Miranda and Ferdinand, they show Iris (the rainbow messenger of the gods) asking Ceres (the goddess of agriculture) and Juno (the wife of Jupiter) to bless the happy couple and celebrate their coming marriage.

- Ariel brings Stephano, Trinculo and Caliban back after the phantom dogs have finished chasing them. Prospero sends them into his cave to put back the clothes they have taken and to tidy up the place. In spite of their plan to kill him and take over the island, Prospero is prepared to pardon them.

Back in time

William Shakespeare was born in 1564 in Stratford-upon-Avon, and later went to London, where he became an actor and playwright. He was very popular in his own lifetime. He wrote thirty-seven plays that we know of, and many sonnets.

The very first theatres were built around the time that Shakespeare was growing up. Until then, plays had been performed in rooms at the back of inns or pubs. The Elizabethans loved going to watch entertainments such as bear-baiting and cock-fighting as well as plays. They also liked to watch public executions, and some of the plays written at this time were quite gruesome.

The Globe, where Shakespeare's company acted, was a round wooden building that was open to the sky in the middle. 'Groundlings' paid a penny to stand around the stage in the central yard. They risked getting wet if it rained. Wealthier people could have a seat in the covered galleries around the edge of the space. Some very important people even had a seat on the stage itself. Unlike today's theatre-goers, Elizabethan audiences were noisy and sometimes fighting broke out.

There were no sets or scene changes in these plays. It was up to the playwright's skill with words to create thunderstorms or forests or Egyptian queens in the imagination of the audience.

Shakespeare wrote mostly in blank verse, in unrhymed lines of ten syllables with a *te-tum te-tum* rhythm. But unlike most writers of his time he tried to make his actors' lines closer to the rhythms of everyday speech, in order to make it sound more naturalistic. He used poetic imagery, and even invented words that we still use today.

His plays are mostly based on stories or old plays that he improved. *The Tempest* may be based on an earlier German play which tells of a magician prince who has a spirit attendant, and an only daughter who falls in love with the son of her father's enemy. There is also a true story from 1609 of a miraculous escape from a shipwreck onto a desert island by a ship's crew sent out from England to America. The news of this event reached England in 1610, a year before *The Tempest* was written.

Finding out more

We recommend the following books and websites to gain a greater understanding of William Shakespeare and Elizabethan England.

Books

- Marcia Williams, *Mr William Shakespeare's Plays*, Walker Books, 2009.

- Alan Durband, *Shakespeare Made Easy: The Tempest*, Nelson Thornes, 1989.

- Leon Garfield, *Shakespeare Stories*, Victor Gollanz, 1985.

- Stewart Ross, *William Shakespeare*, Writers in Britain series, Evans, 1999.

- Dereen Taylor, *The Tudors and the Stuarts*, Wayland, 2007.

Websites

- www.shakespeare.org.uk
Good general introduction to Shakespeare's life.
Contains information and pictures of the houses
linked to him in and around Stratford.

- www.elizabethan-era.org.uk
Lots of information including details of Elizabethan
daily life.

TV and film

- *Shakespeare: The Animated Tales*, DVD
Metrodome Distribution Ltd, 2007.

- *The Tempest*, 1979. Directed by Derek Jarman.

- *The Tempest*, BBC Shakespeare Collection, 1980.
Directed by John Gorrie.

- *Forbidden Planet*, MGM, 1956. Directed by Fred
Wilcox. An American sci-fi film story loosely based
on *The Tempest*.

Food for thought

Here are some things to think about if you are
reading *The Tempest* alone, or ideas for discussion if
you are reading it with friends.

In retelling *The Tempest* we have tried to recreate, as accurately as possible, Shakespeare's original plot and characters. We have also tried to imitate aspects of his style. Remember, however, that this is not the original work; thinking about the points below, therefore, can help you begin to understand William Shakespeare's craft. To move forward from here, turn to the full-length version of *The Tempest* and lose yourself in his wonderful storytelling.

Starting points

● Who do you feel sorry for at the beginning of the play? Why?

● Why do you think Prospero wanted Alonso and his son to be separated after the storm and to think that each other was dead?

● Why might Prospero want Miranda and Ferdinand to fall in love?

● Caliban wanted Stephano and Trinculo to kill Prospero. Why do you think he didn't want to do it himself? Do you think they would have agreed to if they hadn't been drunk?

- Do you think Prospero should have forgiven his enemies? Why do you think he did?

- Could you imagine growing up on a desert island like Miranda did? What would be good about it, and what wouldn't be so good?

Themes

What do you think William Shakespeare is saying about the following themes in *The Tempest*?

- treachery

- hardship and suffering

- reconciliation

Style

Can you find examples of the following?

- a character speaking in prose

- a character speaking in blank verse

- poetic imagery

- a simile (where something is described as being like something else)

- an iambic pentameter (see the next page)

- a rhyming couplet (see below)

Try your hand at writing an iambic (*eye-am-bic*) pentameter. It must have ten syllables arranged in pairs; the first syllable of each pair is unstressed and the second is stressed, like this from *The Tempest*:

I *am* the *best* of *them* that *speak* this *speech*.

Try writing a rhyming couplet, as in Ariel's speech:

Sea nymphs hourly ring his *knell*.
Hark now I hear them. Ding, dong, *bell*.

Something old, something new

In this *Real Reads* version of *The Tempest*, Shakespeare's original words have been interwoven with new linking text in Shakespearean style. If you are interested in knowing which words are original and which new, visit www.realreads.co.uk/shakespeare/ comparison/tempest – here you will find a version with the original words highlighted. It might be fun to guess in advance which are which!